Book Three

of the

by A. J. Atlas
illustrated by Anne Zimanski

Welcome, Readers!

Before you get started, I thought you might like to know a few interesting things about the *Travels with Zozo...*™ series. First of all, the stories are set in real places, so the illustrations you'll see try to show the actual landscapes, plants, and animals found in those locations. Second, the cultural and historical elements you'll read about are also as accurate as possible. I hope this knowledge makes the books even more enjoyable for you.

For this story, the settings are the Great Barrier Reef and Heron Island, Queensland, in Australia.

In a few parts of the story, a teeny bit more creativity and imagination was added. Most of it will be quite obvious, like the golfing crabs. (That cracks me up every time I see it!) Other, less obvious, elements that are not 100% accurate include the following:

- Though bunnies can swim, they have only been seen swimming above the water and for short periods of time. Bunnies cannot breathe underwater.

- Traveling by boat or any vehicle can stress a bunny, especially on an extended trip. However, there is no evidence to show that bunnies get motion sickness.

- The illustrated glass-bottom boat is an original design and probably wouldn't float correctly. The boat would need to be a proper catamaran or have a hull.

- Sea creatures should not be approached, even though Zozo does. It is not safe to go near or try to touch unknown animals.

For the most part, the rest of the information I have presented is accurate and, in my opinion, super interesting! Here are a few more fun facts about Heron Island and the Great Barrier Reef:

- Heron Island is a coral cay situated on Australia's Great Barrier Reef. Heron Island, like other coral cays, formed when ocean currents carried sediment from the reef below and deposited it on a flat point on the reef. Over time, the sediment built up to create the island.

- The Great Barrier Reef is the longest reef in the world. It lies in the Coral Sea, off the coast of Queensland, in northeastern Australia. It is over 1400 miles (2300 kilometers) long and includes more than 900 islands.

And one last thing, two words that might be new to you include:
- Bonzer — BON-zah (Australian word for "excellent, awesome, or first-rate")
- G'day — GUH-day (Australian word for "hello" and a contraction of "good day")

— AJA

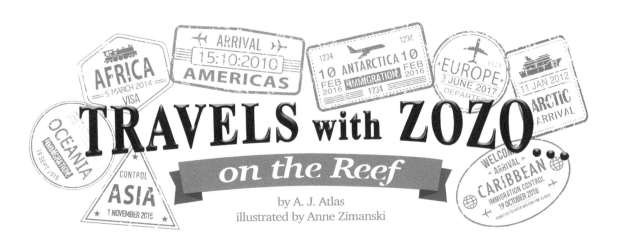

TRAVELS with ZOZO
on the Reef

by A. J. Atlas
illustrated by Anne Zimanski

IMAGINON
BOOKS

Zozo was a hoppity,

floppity,

huggable,

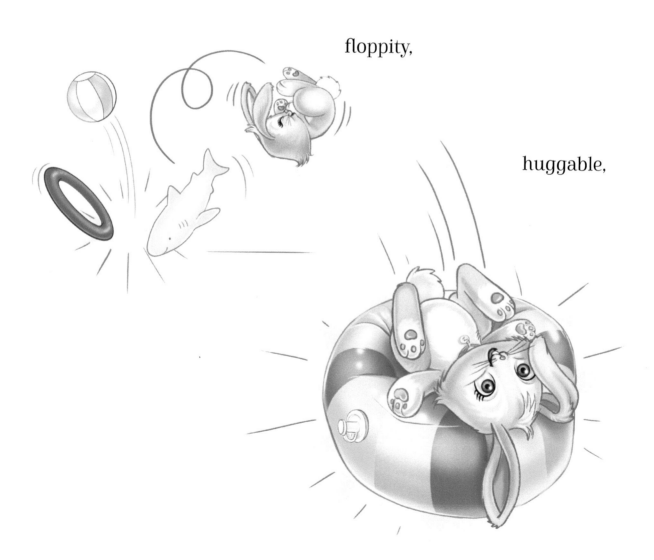

snuggable

pet bunny who **loved** to sleep.

She lived with a fun, on-the-run family of four who loved to travel. Together, they crisscrossed the world sharing adventures and making new friends.

Wherever Zozo and her family were going this time, it was very far from home. Zozo had counted three airplane rides so far. Yet they still weren't there. There was one more flight to go.

It was on a helicopter!

Wow! This is amazing! Zozo thought,
watching the land move further and further
away as they lifted straight up into the sky
and zoomed far out over the ocean.

Soon, Zozo could see only water in all directions.
She inched closer to the window and gazed out. *I've
never seen so many shades of blue in one place before!*
she thought. It was like someone had drawn with
every blue crayon in the big box of crayons, creating
such a pretty sight that Zozo could not stop staring.

Further out to sea, Zozo began to see large patches of brown and gray that appeared scattered under the blue water.

Zozo's brother, Benji, saw them too. "A coral reef!" he exclaimed, lifting Zozo to give her a better view.

Zozo noticed that some parts of the reef were large enough to poke out of the water and create little islands. The helicopter tilted and headed for one of the coral islands.

Zozo and her family had finally made it to their destination.

That night, starlight lit the itty-bitty island on the big, long reef in the vast ocean. The soft sound of waves lapping upon the shore lulled everyone to sleep. *Swish, swish, swish.*

"Time to explore the reef!" announced Zozo's sister, Jazz, rousing her sleepy-headed pet bunny the next morning. She carried Zozo onboard a waiting, glass-bottom boat. Benji, Mom, and Dad followed.

As the boat motored away from the dock into deep ocean water, Zozo's eyes widened in amazement. Through the boat's clear floor, she saw colorful creatures of all shapes and sizes playing in the water beneath her.

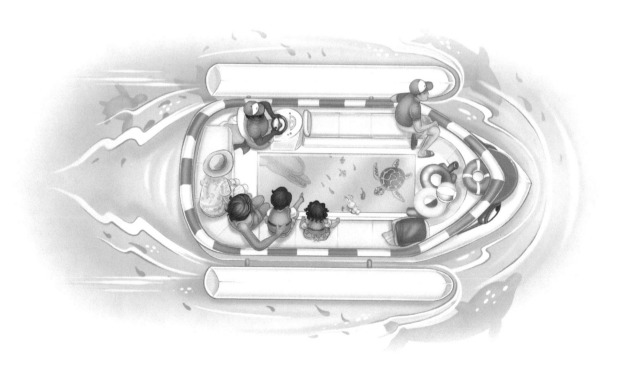

Slowly, though, Zozo's excitement faded. Each time the boat went over a large, rolling wave, the motion made her feel dizzy. She laid down, resting her head between her paws, feeling sick to her stomach.

Mom noticed Zozo looked a bit seasick. "I'm sorry you don't feel well," she said, comforting her with a soft caress. Then, placing a bowl of water down, Mom added, "A little water and some rest should help."

After a few minutes, the boat stopped. Mom, Dad, Benji, and Jazz took turns petting their little bunny. "Feel better," they encouraged her. Then they headed toward the back of the boat, peeling off clothes to reveal their swimsuits.

Zozo flopped her head lazily on the see-through floor. She wished she could go swimming, but she felt too ill.

Suddenly, the boat rocked side-to-side. Water sprayed into the boat, forming puddles. *Must be Mom or Dad jumping in to go for a swim,* Zozo thought.

Again, the boat pitched side-to-side with a much bigger movement. Zozo slid across the bottom of the boat, and *splash*, right into a puddle of water!

The cool water made her feel less dizzy, so she rolled around.

The soft sound of gentle waves lapping up on the side of the swaying boat drifted to her ears. *Swish, swish, swish*...the boat rocked again, and...

...Zozo was swimming! "Yippee!" she exclaimed as she dug her paws in large circles through the water. Her back legs kicked a steady path down, down, down toward the reef.

She didn't know how she could possibly be swimming. But, as two friendly-looking sea turtles smiled up at her and a fan-shaped coral waved, she soon forgot to care. She was having too much fun!

Unexpectedly, Zozo felt herself lifted, as if by a soft, rising carpet.

"G'day, mate!" exclaimed a spotted eagle ray, opening its eyes wide in surprise. "What's a furry, little bunny like you doing swimming in Australia's Great Barrier Reef?"

Before Zozo could say a word, the ray looked ahead at the reef and blurted out, "No worries! The last race is about to start. If we hurry, we can watch it together. This race is for the sharks, whales, and other huge fish in the reef. They're the heavyweights, and you'll love 'em!"

Zozo held tightly, and the two zoomed off toward fish gathering on the far side of a coral wall. Atop the ray, Zozo saw the reef up close for the first time. Tiny, red, polka-dotted seahorses shared the wavy, green seagrass with reddish-brown sea turtles.

Fish of all colors—from pink and orange to silver and blue—wiggled around yellow, brain-shaped coral. *I'd need the entire crayon box full of colors to draw this reef!* she thought.

"This is exciting!" Zozo said cheerfully to the ray, as they slowed and snaked through the crowd looking for the best place to watch the race. Zozo leaned closer and introduced herself, "My name is Zozo. What's yours?"

"Bonzer," the ray answered with a wide grin and a peppy, little, rollercoaster dip through the water. "It means *excellent* or *awesome* to us Australians, so I quite like my name."

"I like it too," Zozo said with a friendly pat on Bonzer's smooth, wing-like fin.

Soon, Bonzer and Zozo positioned themselves in the seagrass at the edge of the raceway.

A moment later, three giant clams closed their shells one after the next, *CLOMP, CLOMP, CLOMP.*

The heavyweight race had begun!

SWOOSH! The racers jetted past the crowd, kicking up a wave in their wake. Zozo's grip on Bonzer slipped. Her back feet flew out from under her. She scrambled to regain her balance. As the unexpected, swirling surge surprised her, she nearly fell off Bonzer. But she recovered her footing and gripped Bonzer more firmly.

"Let's follow them to the finish line," Bonzer urged, swimming out of the seagrass and up above the raceway.

Zozo gazed out across the large reef, listening while Bonzer explained, "These big blokes would race the entire length of the Great Barrier Reef if we'd let them. But it's the world's biggest reef! It would take too long. So, they only race a little ways up here."

From atop Bonzer, Zozo watched the heavyweights jostle for position and fight for the lead. A sailfish nosed ahead, a shark swerved in front, and a ray slid by the pack. Then, in one last effort, a great, gray whale pushed past all the others and won!

"Awesome!
Bonzer!
Fantastic!"
cried the crowd.

Celebrating, the whale swam around in large circles. Then the whale dove straight down. Bonzer, appearing to understand what the whale was about to do, quickly turned to Zozo. "Hold on tight, Zozo!" he warned. "That whale looks keen to leap out of the water!"

Zozo gripped Bonzer just as the whale's flippers effortlessly turned her enormous body upward. Her powerful tail fin propelled her toward the sun-filtered water above them, creating large waves roiling the water near Bonzer and Zozo. Breaking through the surface, into the air above, the whale's great head and half her body rose far out of the water.

"A whale is jumping out of the water!" Zozo heard
Jazz announce.

I know, I know. She's the winner, Zozo thought.
Opening her eyes sleepily, she looked out towards
the water and saw a whale in midair.

The whale turned and splashed back down on its side. Water blasted out in all directions, causing the boat to rock wildly.

Zozo slid across the floor, and *squish*, right into a heap of towels! She looked around, blinking her eyes repeatedly.

"I'm back on the boat," she told herself, looking right, left, up, and down. She settled her gaze on the floor of the boat. Through it, she saw the colorful sea life playing in the reef. Had she really gone swimming with them, or had it all just been a dream?

Still thinking about the racing fish, Zozo yawned and stretched. She peered again through the glass bottom into the water below. Swimming beneath her was a spotted eagle ray. It swam close, seemed to wink, and then swam away. *Bonzer*, Zozo thought, before closing her eyes and letting the waves drift her off to sleep.

Explore Bolivia's wild, wild West in Zozo's next adventure, *Travels with Zozo... on the Salt Flat!*

Travels with Zozo...on the Reef   by A.J. Atlas   illustrated by Anne Zimanski

Published by ImaginOn Books,
an imprint of ImaginOn LLC
www.imaginonbooks.com

1st Edition
2 4 6 8 10 9 7 5 3 1

978-1-954405-03-5 (Hardcover)   978-1-954405-33-2 (Ebook)

Printed
in U.S.A.

To purchase books or obtain more information about the author, illustrator, or upcoming books, visit www.travelswithzozo.com

CPSIA information can be obtained
at www.ICGtesting.com
Printed in the USA
LVHW050230301021
701739LV00004B/30